This book
belongs to

Gillian

friend of the fairies

For Beth

First published by
Zero to Ten Limited
(a member of the Evans Publishing Group)
© 2003 Zero to Ten Limited
Text © 2003 Meg Clibbon
Illustrations © 2003 Lucy Clibbon
Reprinted 2007

British Library Cataloguing in Publication Data

Clibbon, Meg
Fairy Spotter's guide
1. Fairies – Pictorial works – Juvenile literature
I. Title
398.4'5

ISBN 978 1 84089 297 0

Printed and bound in China

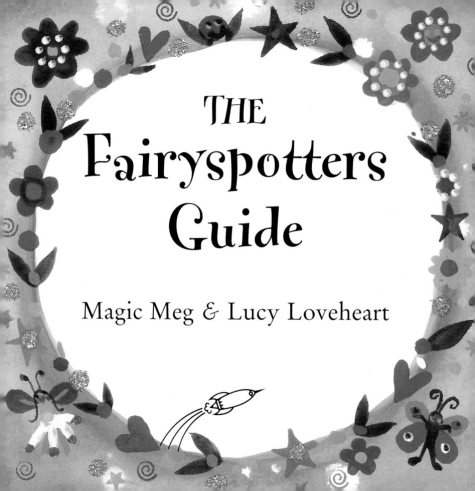

THE Fairyspotters Guide

Magic Meg & Lucy Loveheart

Fairy Queens

On the edge of the Enchanted Forest between Fairyland and the real world are the Arboreal Palaces where the Fairy Queens live. They tell humans about Fairyland and they tell the fairies all about what is happening outside the Enchanted Forest. They are very important, with the best magic wands and wings.

Fairy Princesses

Fairies can become princesses if they have
personality and special skills.
They are generally treated like celebrities,
and they like spending money on themselves.
They are decorative and self-confident and
love shopping for clothes and flowers,
especially sweet peas.

buttercup

daisy

Flower Fairies

Inside each flower lives an invisible fairy
with a personality all of its own.
For example Snowdrop Fairies are very shy,
Buttercup Fairies are very happy, Foxglove
Fairies are mysterious and Marigold Fairies
are quite fierce, which is why people always
plant marigolds in vegetable gardens
to keep off pests.

tulip

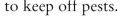

forget-me-not

aquilegia

dandelion

marigold

sunflower

bluebell

foxglove

violet

poppy

hyacinth

snowdrop

Loveheart Fairies

Whenever people feel cross or whenever there is an argument the Loveheart Fairies are needed because these delightful fairies spread love and peace wherever they go. They soothe wounded pride and ruffled feelings and make everyone feel better. They are also very useful members of the Fairy Godmother's Dating Agency.

Angelicas

The Angelicas are so secret that they are
hardly ever seen. Sometimes a sweet
fragrance fills the forest. Sometimes
chiming, tinkling bells ring out from the
treetops. Sometimes the most beautiful
music can be heard which makes the fairies
stop their work just to listen. At such times
you know the Angelicas are close by.

Dream Fairies

Drifting above the Enchanted Forest are fluffy white clouds where the Dream Fairies live. All through the night they catch the dreams of sleeping fairies down below and toss them up to the twinkling stars. Then they wish on them to make the dreams come true.

Footloose Fairies

The Footloose Fairies are sporty, adventurous and energetic. They are full of fun and mischief. The Enchanted Forest rings to the sound of their laughter as they sing and call to each other and play games.

Tinkerbelles

These fairies are quite rare, which is probably
a good thing because they are naughty and if
there is any mischief around there is usually
a Tinkerbelle at the bottom of it. They adore
the wood pixies, especially the boys, and when
these naughty boys and the Tinkerbelles
get together there is trouble ahead!

Rainbow Fairies

Rainbow Fairies are translucent and sparkle
in the air, every one a different colour,
their wings tipped with indigo. Each one of
these fairies brings hope and joy to anyone
lucky enough to see them and they are
always around at fairy parties.

Housework Fairies

If there is a toadstool to polish or fairy dust to sweep up
or windows to clean with gossamer then the Housework
Fairies are there ready to help. They fly in and out
without fuss or noise and where they have been
everywhere is fresh and gleaming.

Jewel Fairies

Jewel Fairies are the colours of amethyst, sapphire, ruby, emerald and all the other gem stones. They sparkle like diamonds in the sunlight and glow like opals in the moonlight. Their job is to turn precious jewels into fairy dust with all the other magical ingredients.

Fairy Godmothers

Wise and clever fairies are sometimes
chosen to be Fairy Godmothers or
Fairy Godfathers and have to have special
training because they live so close to humans.
When they come back to the Enchanted
Forest they help to teach the little fairies the
lore of fairyland and how to slide down
moonbeams into the land of dreams.

Herb Fairies

These are the medicine fairies because they
live in herbs and know all about their healing
properties. Herb Fairies are green and gold
and you always know they are there
because of their fragrance. Being near a
Herb Fairy makes you feel better but if you
are really ill they prepare special mixtures
or perfumed oils to make you well.

Tea Fairies

Some people think that these are the
best fairies of all. There is nothing like a
nice cup of tea at the right time to make
you feel good and the Tea Fairies know
this. They may not look the prettiest or be
the most magical fairies, but the world
would be a poorer place without them.

Grandma Fairies

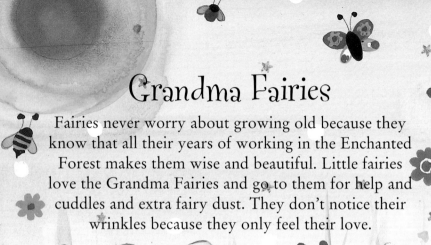

Fairies never worry about growing old because they know that all their years of working in the Enchanted Forest makes them wise and beautiful. Little fairies love the Grandma Fairies and go to them for help and cuddles and extra fairy dust. They don't notice their wrinkles because they only feel their love.

Tooth Fairies

Although nobody can see the Tooth Fairies, children
know all about them because if they hide their baby
teeth under their pillows, they are gone in the
morning and some money is left behind instead.
The Tooth Fairies fly with the teeth back to Fairyland
where they are ground up to become part of Fairy Dust.

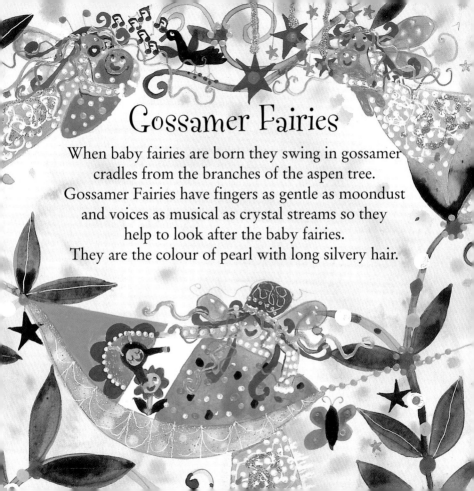

Gossamer Fairies

When baby fairies are born they swing in gossamer
cradles from the branches of the aspen tree.
Gossamer Fairies have fingers as gentle as moondust
and voices as musical as crystal streams so they
help to look after the baby fairies.
They are the colour of pearl with long silvery hair.

Party Fairies

There are so many occasions when fairies have parties, that the Party Fairies are always busy – writing invitations on rose petals, arranging the toadstools in the fairy ring, organising the Housework Fairies, the Rainbow Fairies and the Tea Fairies and doing all the other things.